Little, Brown and Company
Hachette Book Group
1290 Avenue of the Americas, New York, NY 10104
Visit us at lb-kids.com
mylittlepony.com

First Edition: August 2017

Little, Brown and Company is a division of Hachette Book Group, Inc. The Little, Brown name and logo are trademarks of Hachette Book Group, Inc.

The publisher is not responsible for websites (or their content) that are not owned by the publisher.

Library of Congress Control Number 2017938356

ISBNs: 978-0-316-55765-8 (pbk.),
978-0-316-55764-1 (hardcover), 978-0-316-55762-7 (ebook)

Printed in the United States of America

LSC-C

10 9 8 7 6 5 4 3 2 1

THE JUNIOR NOVEL

Adapted by G. M. Berrow
Based on a Screenplay written by
Meghan McCarthy and Rita Hsiao
Produced by Brian Goldner and Stephen Davis
Directed by Jayson Thiessen

Little, Brown and Company
New York • Boston

In the magical land of Equestria, there ruled four powerful pony princesses. One for the day, one for the night, one for love, and, last but not least, one to represent the magic of a force greater than any other—friendship. That pony was named Princess Twilight Sparkle, and she was incredibly special.

Though Twilight Sparkle had just recently ascended to her role as princess, everypony knew she was wise beyond her years. However, Princess Twilight herself acknowledged she still had much to learn. But luckily, lessons were not just a very serious business to her—they were *everything*. In fact, that's how Twilight had already come to understand that it was her supreme royal duty to make everypony feel as if they belonged.

Thanks to her amazing friends, who taught her how to embody and practice this skill, Twilight felt that she was well prepared to meet whatever friendship challenge lay ahead of her and the citizens of Equestria. Pinkie Pie, Rarity, Rainbow Dash, Fluttershy, and Applejack would be there for Twilight—no matter what!

It was Twilight's greatest wish that everypony in Equestria would experience the Magic of Friendship. It was such a relief to have somepony with whom to laugh, share time, practice loyalty, show kindness, and offer an honest opinion. Sometimes Twilight Sparkle thought holding such an esteemed position could feel like a lot of pressure. But as long as Princess Twilight had her friends and a well-thought-out plan, she knew, deep in her royal heart, she would be the princess everypony needed her to be.

But even the ever-prepared Princess Twilight would soon learn a new lesson—there are simply some things that nopony could plan for.

CHAPTER ONE

The painted purple-and-pink sunrise melted into cool, breezy blue skies as ponies from all over Equestria journeyed toward the bustling epicenter of Canterlot. Hundreds of winged Pegasi soared through the fluffy clouds up above. Down below, the Unicorns and Earth ponies journeyed by train, cart, and hoof from the far reaches of the kingdom.

The excitement for the inaugural event was so palpable that it seemed as if it were buzzing through the air in little shock waves. Some ponies even felt butterflies in their tummies and sweet songs on their lips as they anticipated all the fun and friendship they were going to experience at the very first Festival of Friendship. Anything could happen.

The busy streets were starting to fill up as Spike, the young Dragon who acted as best friend (and adviser) to the Princess of Friendship, pushed his way with urgency through the gathering crowds. "Excuse me!" he called out, struggling to keep hold of the armloads of important scrolls he was taking to the princess. "Dragon on the move! Comin' through! Watch your tail!" Ponies darted out of the way to accommodate him, whispering with excitement as he passed.

"What do you even *do* at a Friendship Festival?" an Earth pony with red pigtails commented in awe as she took in the glorious scene around her.

"Make friends, bond over music...meet all four princesses?!" a golden-colored mare with a honeypot cutie mark replied as they trotted off to find out.

Spike took mental note of their excited comments so he could relay to Princess Twilight how wonderful an idea the whole festival had been. It hadn't even started yet, and it was already a hit! Spike just knew it was going to be thrilling—he had a feeling in his gut.

The little Dragon continued across the cobblestoned plaza with his scrolls, a happy pep in his steps. He was so distracted, he almost walked right into a pair of overexcited filly Pegasi flying right past him and up into the air. Their giggles of delight were even louder than those of the ponies jumping in the bouncy castle.

"Do you think they'll let me wear their crowns?" wondered a lilac filly named Violet Petals as she soared high above Canterlot to get a better view.

Her friend grinned. "I bet Princess Twilight is the most perfect pony *ever*!"

It seemed that everypony had the beloved princesses on their minds. Besides the appearance of the royal princesses, so many exciting things were still to be seen! But the true mane event of the weekend would be the stunning musical styling of the super-talented Songbird Serenade. The pop star was set to perform in an epic show that would undoubtedly go down in Equestrian history as one of the best of all time.

Or it *might*, depending on whether Twilight could persuade the other princesses to go along with her ingenious plan to enhance the experience for everypony in the audience.

Up in the castle, Twilight paced tirelessly...and more than a little nervously. She couldn't stop fretting over the fact that every detail of the occasion had to be just perfect. After all, everypony's happiness rested in Twilight's hooves! She couldn't let them down.

Taking a cue from her own serene image depicted in the stained-glass windows, Twilight paused and spread her majestic purple wings out wide. She took a deep breath to summon her courage and center her thoughts. Twilight held the air in her lungs for a moment. *Just go in there and ask*, she told herself. *This is your Friendship Festival.*

She expelled the air in a heavy sigh and shook her head in frustration. "Nope! Still worried. *Oooh...* nothing is working!" She let her face fall into her hoof and scrunched her muzzle. Luckily, a friendly voice pulled her from her thoughts.

"Okay, Twilight!" Spike scrambled inside the cavernous hall with a smirk on his face. He was still buzzing from all the activity outside. "Got all your charts and graphs!" The Dragon carried his mountain of scrolls to the princess.

"Oh, thank goodness you're here, Spike!" Twilight called out. "I'm just so nervous about this meeting."

"Just remember the most important thing," he assured her.

"To smile?!" Twilight twisted her face into a forced version of one.

"Uh, no..." he replied, a little scared by her over-the-top intensity. "You have a *plan*."

"Yes, that's true." Twilight nodded. Of course Spike was right. Twilight had prepared for this, and there was nothing to be afraid of. The other three princesses knew her well. Whatever she had to say, they would listen. Twilight was ready. She nodded at Spike and stepped through the massive double doors to the throne room.

"Wish me luck!"

CHAPTER TWO

The three other royals listened intently as Twilight enthusiastically bounded back and forth in front of her large whiteboard, which showed an illustration of the performance stage alongside several very advanced friendship equations. If Twilight could get the other princesses to agree to this minor adjustment, it would ensure that the Friendship Festival would be the most wonderful event that Equestria had ever seen!

"Songbird Serenade's performance is not scheduled to start until after you begin the sunset, and based on my precise calculation, to get the very best lighting for the stage"—Twilight looked to Princess Celestia—"I was hoping you could make sure the sun stays about twenty-eight point one degrees to the south," Twilight said as she drew a little Celestia on the board underneath a picture of the sun. Her voice seemed to speed up once she got started.

"And, Princess Luna, if you could raise the moon sixty-two degrees to the north at the same time, it would reflect the sunlight on the other side and really frame the entire stage perfectly!" Twilight drew a picture of Luna underneath the moon and an acute angle to prove that her theory was sound.

Princesses Celestia and Luna looked at each other in disbelief. Why did their fellow princess stress herself out over such minor details? Luna opened her mouth to reply, but Twilight wasn't finished just yet.

"And, Cadance, if you could use your crystal magic to create an aurora above the stage, the sun *and* the moon will shine through it and create a truly amazing light show!"

As Twilight spoke her final words, Spike threw a claw-ful of glitter up into the air. It swirled down as if it were a beautiful aurora. Spike then poked a hoofmade paper puppet of the pop star above the whiteboard and made it dance. "Presenting Songbird Serenade! *Yaaaa, yaaah! Whoaa ho ho!*" Spike leaped on top of the board for emphasis but quickly lost his balance. The Dragon tumbled to the ground.

Twilight blushed at Spike's awkward display and opened her wings to block the princesses' view of him. She flashed a toothy smile to punctuate her brilliant presentation. Any minute now they would congratulate her and...

"So you're saying you want us to move the sun and the moon..." Princess Luna recapped, a hesitant look on her face, "for the *party*?"

"Well, I'd do it myself." Twilight laughed nervously. "But I don't have your magic!"

It was difficult to gauge their thoughts, but the fact that all three princesses stepped toward her with their horns glowing gave Twilight a little glimmer of hope. But Princess Celestia just frowned. "Twilight, each of us uses our powers to serve Equestria in our own way." Celestia's face softened as she reached for Twilight's chin with her gold-plated hoof. "You are the Princess of Friendship! You already have all the magic you need."

"So...that'd be a no?" Twilight sighed in defeat. How was she going to make the festival special now? She could feel her disappointment sinking in, but before it had the chance, her trusty pal Spike snapped into action. He pushed her out of the throne room. After all, they had a checklist to get to and ponies to see. There was no time to waste today!

Everypony was waiting for her.

CHAPTER THREE

The last few stubborn clouds above Canterlot were obliterated with a single swoop from Rainbow Dash. The Pegasus sped through each one with glee and watched as her rainbow trail broke through the mist. Rainbow Dash loved clearing the skies, but she loved helping her friends even more. To do both at once was her favorite!

"Skies cleared and ready for the festival!" Rainbow Dash announced with satisfaction. She took off toward the main plaza, where a vast amphitheater was being decorated for the evening's events. Maybe somepony needed a hoof with something else!

"That looks awesome, Pinkie!" Rainbow Dash

shouted as she swooped past Pinkie Pie. The pink party pony was busy blowing up balloons and twisting them into fun shapes. Pinkie took a deep breath and blew into a red balloon with all her might. It inflated quickly and a few seconds later she had turned it into a perfect likeness of Discord. But before she could admire her hoofiwork, the balloon sprung a leak and shot off into the distance.

"Heads up! *RUNAWAY BALLOON!*" Pinkie Pie squealed as she bounded after the fugitive straight past Fluttershy, who was busy preparing for the festival. The sweet yellow Pegasus spun around in surprise as her singing flock of chorus birds took flight in every direction.

Nearby, Applejack was busy hauling her apple-cider cart through the courtyard, giving out free samples to anypony she came across. After passing out a few mugs to grateful ponies, she trotted over to the stage area to check on its progress. Unsurprisingly, Rarity was keeping herself busy by delicately hanging bows along the edge. After she tied each one, she used her magic to place a beautiful gem in the center of it. The stage was beginning to look exactly as Rarity hoped it would—perfect.

"Wow, Rarity, that's a fine job you're doin' there!" Applejack shouted to her meticulous friend. "Course, it might not get done till *after* the concert!" Rarity had hung only three bows so far.

"Applejack, darling, anypony can do a 'fine' job." Rarity turned up her muzzle and closed her eyes. "Twilight asked me, so clearly she's going for 'fabulous'! And fabulous takes time." The Unicorn got back to work, carefully tying the next bow with love.

"Fabulous takes forever!" Rainbow Dash butted in as she landed near Applejack. "But *'awesome'*? That can get done in four seconds flat!" Before Rarity could protest, Rainbow Dash darted over to her and grabbed the ribbons and gems. She zoomed around the stage in the blink of an eye. When the ponies looked again, the entire thing was finished!

Rainbow Dash grinned. "I could do it even faster if

I did my Sonic Rainboom...." she said proudly. But it looked awful. The bows drooped, and the gems were misplaced.

Rarity cried out in despair. How was she going to fix this mess in time? "No, no, no! Don't you dare! It looks wretched enough already—"

Rainbow Dash shrugged. "Oh, come on, it looks fine."

"If you were raised in a barn!" Rarity huffed. "No offense, Applejack."

"None taken!" Applejack laughed good-naturedly and kept pouring mugs of cider. Her family just happened to have a barn. Where she was born. And spent most of her formative years.

Rarity rushed over to the mess and began to fix it. Fluttershy and Pinkie Pie trotted up to help, but before they could, everypony noticed that Twilight and Spike were approaching. They were hidden behind a huge scroll with a checklist on it, which meant the friends were probably at peak pre-event stress levels.

"Hey, Twilight!" everypony chorused cheerily.

Rarity smirked at the little Dragon. "Hello, Spike."

Spike waved back and blushed pink with embarrass-ment. After all this time, he still had a crush on the glamorous pony.

"How'd it go with the other princesses?" Applejack smiled brightly. "They like your idea?"

"Not exactly." Twilight sighed heavily, reliving the meeting and feeling just as bad all over again. "They think I can make today perfect *without* their magic."

"And they are absolutely right, darling!" Rarity moved closer to Twilight. She just needed some extra support. "This festival is your brilliant idea, and we all know you're up to the task!" Rarity assured her.

Twilight bit her lip, unconvinced. But what if she wasn't? What if Songbird Serenade hated the stage? Or nopony made a new friend? If she failed at the fes-tival, then who was she? Not the Princess of Friend-ship, that's for sure.

"Twilight!" Pinkie Pie bounded over and took Twi-light's face in her hooves. "Look at me!" Pinkie's stare was all sorts of intense, and her bushy fuchsia mane sprung out wildly. "This will be the biggest celebration

Equestria has ever seen! You *cannot* fail. The pressure is *intense*! It's almost too much for any single pony to handle...!" Pinkie squealed. She really wasn't helping Twilight's nerves.

"But you have us!" Pinkie finished with a cheesy smile. She gestured to Rainbow Dash, Fluttershy, Rarity, and Applejack. "So stop worrying."

Twilight's friends gathered around her and enveloped her in a group hug. *"We got this!"* they all shouted together before erupting into a fit of giggles. Twilight smiled in spite of herself. With the help of her friends, she'd have no problem getting everything just right. All they had to do was make it fun!

Applejack started to hum a tune. Soon enough, everypony was singing along together as they worked to ready everything from the epic stage to the decorations, the food, and the games.

"We got this....We got this together!" Twilight sang along as she trotted past the booths. It was finally beginning to feel as if the forecast would be nothing but sunny skies and a perfect festival, when all of a sudden...

SPLAT! Twilight found herself encased in the middle of a gigantic, sugary, buttery, fluffy, colorful... cake? *"Pinkie!"* Twilight whined, stepping out of the gooey mess. Dollops of frosting and sprinkles slid down her mane and wings, and a single lit birthday candle had landed precisely on her horn.

"Oopsie! Guess my easy-bake-confetti-cake cannon needs a little more fine-tuning!" Pinkie laughed, popping out of a giant contraption. The ponies who had gathered around gasped in shock.

But the glances and gasps from the crowd weren't directed at Twilight at all—they were for somepony even more special. The star of the show!

CHAPTER FOUR

Songbird Serenade! She's here!" the ponies whispered in awe as the crowd parted to make way for the singer. Her two bodyguard stallions, outfitted in dark jackets and sunglasses, trotted ahead to clear the path even more. They puffed up their chests with a sense of pride and stepped aside. There she was!

The pop diva, a buttercream-colored Earth pony, wore her signature manestyle in black-and-yellow choppy locks that hung directly over her eyes. She had a large pink bow behind her head and a black jacket that was effortlessly cool. Everypony always loved how mysterious her edgy look made her seem.

"Hiya!" Songbird chirped in a sweet voice. "I'm

looking for the pony in charge?" She scanned the crowd aimlessly, looking around at the masses of gawking ponies. "I need to set up for my sound check?"

"Songbird Serenade?" Twilight stepped forward, feeling a bit starstruck. But clearly she should be the one to handle this. On top of everything else. "Um, I was just going to check on you—I'm Princess Twilight!" A gooey blob of cake slid down her shoulder. Suddenly, Twilight was hyperaware of how odd her current state must look to her guest. "And sorry about the mess! Usually, I'm not so—" Twilight gestured, and a drop of batter managed to fling itself right onto Songbird Serenade.

"Caked in...cake?" Songbird laughed as her body-guard wiped it away. Now Twilight was *officially* embarrassed. What else could go wrong today?

A low rumble rang out, and a mass of black and gray started to appear in the sky. "Storm clouds?" cried Twilight. All the good feelings from the past hour were dissipating. "But I ordered perfect weather!" She looked to Rainbow Dash in confusion. The Pegasi had supposedly been working nonstop to make sure no weather catastrophes could possibly ruin their day. "Rainbow Dash?"

"Uh, I . . ." Rainbow Dash's voice quavered. "I don't think those are storm clouds." The masses of ponies watched in bewilderment as a giant airship burst through the darkened mist. It was shaped like a giant egg but had a wooden undercarriage like the hull of a boat. Sharp, angular propellers jutted out from the back, with a rudder below. It was most unusual.

"Oooh!" said Pinkie Pie with glee. "I bet those are the clowns I ordered!"

But as the ship landed on the plaza, it began to crush everything in its path, including several of the strong, tall spires that bore Canterlot's flags. Ponies galloped out of the way to make room for the monstrosity. And Pinkie Pie came to realize the scary airship was definitely *not* holding the clowns she had ordered.

It was something sinister.

Twilight narrowed her eyes, trying to make sense of what was happening. She had a horrible feeling but felt powerless. She didn't even know who these visitors were—so how could she stop them?

Up on the castle balcony, the other princesses experienced the same sinking sensation.

A door on the hull opened, and a gangway unfurled. Silhouetted in its frame was a small, squat creature. Nopony knew it yet, but his name was Grubber. From his pallid gray skin to his piglike nose, up to his white spiky hair and right to the tips of his pointy claws—he was an unusual sight. Grubber hoisted a large box in front of him and made his way down the gangway toward the ponies, trying to look as intimidating as possible.

Once he'd arrived at the bottom of the gangway, Grubber made a big show about pushing a button to open the box. Everypony held their breath as the box grew into a giant mechanical megaphone. Grubber held the cone up to his mouth with satisfaction and, pausing for dramatic effect, summoned his scariest voice.

"Ponies of Equestria…we come on behalf of the fearsome, the powerful, the almighty… *Storm King*!"

Grubber gestured to the ship dramatically, and a giant poster unrolled. On it was a terrifying, horned beast with icy blue eyes. An emblem that looked like two sharp spikes was emblazoned on his chest. Nothing about this intrusion seemed friendly. The ponies erupted into a wave of panicked whispers.

"And now, to deliver his evil, evil message, put your hooves together for *Commander Tempest!*" A proud Grubber looked ecstatic as he gestured with his stubby arm to the door and stepped aside to make way for his superior.

A striking pony stepped forward to reveal herself. Tempest Shadow's dark-purple hide and cropped magenta mane was complemented by her intimidating black armor. The armor was adorned with the same sinister emblem as on the massive poster, right where a pony's cutie mark should be. A mysterious scar marked her right aqua-colored eye. But the strangest feature of all was her horn.

It was *broken.*

At first, Twilight Sparkle wasn't even sure Tempest

was a Unicorn. She'd never seen anypony's horn jutting out into shards like that. Something horrible had happened to her, and Twilight found herself wondering what it was.

"Tempest, is it?" Princess Celestia's gentle yet commanding voice rang out as the three remaining princesses soared down from the castle balcony to greet the intruders. "How may we help you?"

"Ah, I'm so glad you asked." Tempest smirked. Her voice dripped with sarcasm. "How about we start with your complete and *total* surrender?"

CHAPTER FIVE

Twilight pushed past the other ponies and stepped forward to line up with Celestia, Luna, and Cadance. There had to be a diplomatic way to solve this little misunderstanding. All it would take was a friendly conversation, and they'd be back to getting ready for the festival.

"Hi there! Princess of Friendship here." Twilight tried to catch Tempest's eyes. When she did, she felt an icy chill go down her spine. "Not exactly sure what's going on, but I know we can talk things out." Twilight gave her friendliest smile. It always worked.

But Tempest Shadow just chuckled. "Oh goodie. All the princesses!" Tempest started down the gangway, her hoofs striking the metal planks with confidence. "Here's the deal, ladies: I need your magic. Give it up nicely, please, or we will make it difficult." Tempest shot Twilight a pointed look. "For *everyone*."

"And why exactly should we cower before you?" Princess Luna shot back. "There's one of you, and hundreds of us!" Luna gestured to the crowd of ponies behind her, who all puffed out their chests and stood a little taller in support.

Tempest was unfazed. The Unicorn let out a low chuckle. "I was hoping you'd choose...difficult."

Out of nowhere, dozens more of the strange airships appeared in the sky! Hordes of enormous, long-tailed, yeti-like creatures wearing the Storm King's emblem came leaping out of their ships. They grunted and growled as they landed across the Canterlot plaza amid the pastel ponies. The ponies screamed in horror as they ran for cover. Canterlot was under attack!

Cadance sprang into action, lunging toward Tempest's ship. But she was too late. Tempest jumped into the air, spun around, and kicked something with her back hoof. The glowing orb shot straight at Cadance. She was able to block it with her magic shield, but the orb was too strong. It lingered, frozen right in front of Princess Cadance's face as she fought to hold it back.

"I can't…stop it!" Cadance cried out. A moment later, the orb worked its evil magic on the princess, turning her completely into stone. Twilight gasped in horror as Celestia cried out for her fallen comrade.

"Luna! Quick!" Celestia shouted to her sister. "Go south! Beyond the Badlands! Seek help from the Queen of the Hippo—"

But before Celestia could finish her sentence, Tempest had kicked another orb right at the princesses. *"Nooooo!"* Twilight shouted helplessly as stone engulfed Celestia's body. Now she, too, had become a statue, her face contorted in a permanent expression of horror. Luna took off through the air, swerving between the airships to escape and carry out Celestia's instructions.

But it was in vain, because Tempest was a step ahead of Luna. She procured two more glowing green orbs and jumped into the air again, kicking one right at Luna. When it hit her wing, the princess lost control. Luna tumbled back to the ground, and by the time she reached it, she was completely frozen in stone.

Twilight couldn't believe her eyes. All three of the other princesses were immobilized. *"Nooooo!"* She couldn't help crying out in agony.

Tempest cackled, zeroing in on Twilight. One more princess to go before she had what she needed to please the Storm King. She watched as the sweet purple princess was caught in her tracks and overcome with emotion. Too simple.

It was the perfect time to strike. Tempest kicked the last orb at the pony with unbridled glee. An explosion of green smoke and rainbows burst forth, obstructing the view as it hit the sad little pony.

"Easy as pie," Tempest mumbled to herself with certain smugness.

"Oh, I love pie," added Grubber, licking his lips.

The smoke cleared, and Tempest trotted up to the pony frozen in place. Grubber scrambled over and leaned in close to look at her horn. It wasn't a horn at all—it was a party hat! This pony was a cross-eyed Pegasus with a cutie mark of bubbles.

"That's not the princess!" Tempest growled. Her broken horn sputtered and sparked with magical rage. "Grubber...Get. Her. *NOW!*" Grubber panicked and took off toward the edge of the courtyard where Storm Creatures were lunging after a group of ponies.

"Over here, y'all!" Applejack shouted, leading the way.

Rainbow Dash darted ahead—she knew a shortcut out of Canterlot. "Come on!" Fluttershy, Pinkie Pie, Rarity, and Twilight galloped after them, Spike in tow, darting out of the path of the terrifying Storm Creatures every few seconds until they found themselves cornered on a bridge. A creature was blocking their way out!

In a moment of quick thinking, Twilight pointed her horn and fired a magic beam directly at him. He lifted his shield. The magic bounced back and shot directly at the ground. The ponies gasped as a crack began to form in the stone bridge. It was crumbling right beneath their hooves!

The bridge gave way, taking all six ponies and Spike down with it. They screamed as they plunged into the rushing water below. The ponies bobbed to the surface, paddling their hooves and gasping for air, but the current was too strong.

They were headed right for a steep waterfall, and there was no way to stop or avoid it. *"Ahhhhh!"* the friends screamed in unison as they plummeted over the precipice to certain doom.

CHAPTER SIX

The ponies had taken shelter in a tiny cave next to the river below Canterlot. Everypony was wet and bedraggled but seemed to be all right. "Everypony okay?" Applejack asked as she fished her soaking cowpony hat out of the water. The limp brown brim dripped onto her mane.

"We just got our cupcakes handed to us by the worst party crasher *ever*!" Pinkie Pie marveled. She wrung her curly mane, and a bucket's worth of water came pouring out.

Everypony agreed on that point, but nopony could decide what the best next course of action would be. Rainbow Dash wanted to go back and fight, but

Spike insisted that the sheer size and number of the Storm Creatures would make it impossible. Always the practical one, Applejack pointed out that they had to decide quickly—they couldn't just stay in the cave forever. And they couldn't let Tempest Shadow find Twilight. As discussion turned to theories about what might have happened to the evil Unicorn's broken horn, Twilight trotted to the water's edge to think.

Everything had come crashing down so fast. What was she supposed to do now? The kingdom was under occupation, and she was the only princess who'd escaped. It was up to her to rescue everypony! Suddenly, Twilight's mind replayed the events for her, and she remembered a clue.

Celestia had been telling Luna to seek help from somepony. "The queen..." Twilight mumbled to herself.

"Yeah, the queen!" chirped Pinkie Pie, then her face fell. "Uh... what queen?"

"The Queen of the... Hippos?" Twilight replied. When she said it out loud, it sounded ridiculous even to her.

"Hippos?" Rainbow Dash scoffed. "Seriously?"

Twilight nodded. "They're somewhere south, past the Badlands."

Fluttershy cowered. "That means we'll have to…leave Equestria!" Her voice was so tiny it was practically a squeak.

"I'm not even packed!" Rarity whimpered, thinking of all the situations she might find herself in without the proper outfit. She shuddered.

"I understand you're scared. And nopony else has to go…." Twilight replied. She glanced up to the sky, where the airships were still hovering. Thinking of the citizens left in Canterlot made her stomach lurch. "But I have to find this queen. She might be our only hope to save Equestria." Twilight took a deep breath and turned on her hooves to leave. She had no choice. If her friends didn't come, she would just have to go it alone.

"Well, you're not getting all the glory!" Rainbow Dash chimed in. "We're in this together!" The rainbow Pegasus flew over to Twilight and gave her an encouraging smile. The others gathered around and nodded in agreement.

The princess felt a wave of relief wash over her as she realized her friends were all going to be behind her on the journey. She hadn't let herself admit that she had been scared to be alone. Now all they had to do was find out which direction was south.

"Uh...that way?" Spike pointed his claw toward the edge of a forest, thick with wide-trunked trees.

"Let's go find this Hippo. Boingy! Boingy! Boingy!" Pinkie Pie bounced over in her signature style and took the lead. "Hey—anypony up for a game of I Spy?" The others groaned and trotted after her, bracing themselves for the potentially long journey ahead. At least they had one another.

CHAPTER SEVEN

Back in Canterlot, things had gotten worse than Twilight could even imagine. The Storm Creature warriors had rounded up everypony in the whole capital into groups, and then they'd shackled their hooves together. As the Storm King's prisoners, the little ponies were forced to march back and forth endlessly. It was miserable.

Tempest Shadow had taken up residence in the castle. She watched the activity from a balcony, thinking of all the changes that would have to be made to the city once the Storm King finally arrived to take power. Remnants of the Friendship Festival that had never been still littered the sparkly cobblestoned streets, and colorful balloons floated into the air.

"All this power," Tempest mumbled in disgust as a bunch of rainbow-colored balloons floated past her perch, "*wasted* on parties, when there are far greater uses." Tempest could feel the anger rising inside her as she caught her reflection in a pane of glass. Her broken horn stared back at her, ugly and diminished. Tempest pushed her feelings down, rolled her eyes, and trotted back inside the castle. There was work to do.

One of the Storm Creatures stationed as a castle guard approached Tempest. He reached out his claws to her and presented a round glass bottle filled with a glowing liquid. It pulsated with light and emitted a watery, high-pitched sound that echoed through the cavernous hall.

"Well, answer it!" Tempest barked. Sometimes she couldn't help feeling as though she was surrounded by incompetent oafs. They couldn't even accomplish the simplest tasks, like answering a potion call. The Storm Creature fumbled to uncork the bottle and poured it into a large basin. Instantly, the liquid shot up into a vapory cylinder. In the mist, the image of the Storm King appeared.

The frightening beast spun around in confusion. "Where am I supposed to be looking? I never understand how this spell works. *Tempest!*" the Storm King growled.

"Over here, Your Excellency," Tempest said patiently. She was used to her boss relying on her to accomplish even the smallest things. The Storm King was still spinning around, unable to locate her. "Over here, look to your right. Yep."

"Oh, there you are. Here's the deal..." The Storm King waved his gnarled wooden staff at her. The crystal embedded at the top glinted in the projection's light. "Going by the name 'Storm King' is intensely intimidating and everything, but you know what? I need to back it up!" He sneered.

"You know what I need to back it up with? *A storm!*" His icy blue eyes bore into Tempest's. "You promised me magic that could control the elements, and right now I'm holding a what?" The Storm King held up his staff. "A branch, *a twig*! *Blehhh!*"

For the hundredth time, Tempest explained to her superior that he was not, in fact, holding a twig, but the Staff of Sacanas. The ancient relic would serve as a conduit to channel the magic of the four rulers of Equestria. "You'll soon have the power of a hundred armies."

The Storm King smirked. "So that would be a yes on your locking down the four Pegacornicuses, or whatever you call them?"

Tempest braced herself to tell him the bad news— she was still missing one princess. They needed all four of the royals for the staff to work, but that sneaky little purple one had gotten away. Grubber had really messed that one up.

"Give me three days," Tempest decided to say instead of telling the truth. "I'll have everything ready for your arrival." She bowed to the Storm King, and he disappeared into the mist.

Tempest Shadow took a deep breath as she realized the challenge ahead of her. She had better find that pony and fast. Nothing was as important as that. Finding that princess was Tempest's only chance of getting back the thing she desired most from the only creature who could give it to her. Because once he had the power of Equestria in his control, the Storm King was going to restore Tempest's broken horn, and her magic would return with it. Finally.

"Prepare my ship!" Tempest growled at her underlings. Her chipped horn sparked with tiny colored shocks of lightning. Then she narrowed her eyes, determined. "Please, how far can one little pony get on her own?"

CHAPTER EIGHT

The ponies were delirious as they trudged across the barren desert landscape, barely moving at all. The hot sun bore down on their hides. They were dusty, achy, and so thirsty they couldn't remember what water tasted like. They had already come so far. Drops of salty sweat poured down their muzzles, and their eyes were ringed with the dark circles of deep exhaustion. It felt as if Twilight Sparkle and her friends had been trotting their whole lives.

"Saving Equestria!" Pinkie Pie laughed to herself maniacally. "Oh, look!" She plucked an ancient bird skull from the dunes; sand poured from its eye sockets. "Maybe this guy knows which way to go!" Pinkie held the skull to her ear. "What's that? We're lost?!" She tossed the skull and erupted into a fit of fanatical giggles before collapsing into a sandy dune.

Nearby, Spike was struggling with a wayward prickly cactus that had adhered itself to his bottom. "We could be going in circles! Endless sand…nothing for miles but sand"—Spike coughed and sputtered, his throat was so dry—"and this road."

"A road?" said Twilight Sparkle, perking up. "Where there's a road, there's a—" She trotted forward, cresting the nearest dune. What she saw next took her breath away. There was a city!

Klugetown was unlike any city Twilight had ever seen, stacked high with dark, smoking spires and foreign buildings. Even the path to the city looked ominous, littered with old wreckage that jutted out from the sand. But it was something.

"*Oooh!* A city!" Pinkie Pie bounded forward with renewed energy. "We are *doing it*, you guys!" she squealed in delight. The other ponies rushed forward to join her, wondering aloud what sort of amenities might await them. Rarity was hoping for a spa, but everypony else was just eager to rest, find some food, and gather information on where to find the Queen of the Hippos.

But as soon as they entered the main gates of Klugetown, it became instantly clear that this was not the sort of place a pony wanted to find herself alone. The group stuck close to one another, anxiously alert to the strange sights and sounds. Creatures who looked like giant rhinoceroses, beastly hogs, and prickly porcupines grunted as they hawked mysterious goods from their vendor stalls.

Other townsfolk emerged from shadows to peek at and greedily taunt the candy-colored equines as they passed. "That's a lovely horn.... How much?" a cloaked monster whispered to Rarity as she trotted along. Rarity's face contorted in horror at the very thought of selling her horn. Across the way, a tower of spiky-beaked birds in cages squawked at Fluttershy as she neared them. They were scary-looking, but Fluttershy couldn't imagine what sort of beasts thought it okay to trap the poor little babies!

Twilight searched the perilous streets for a friendly face. Anycreature would do, just as long as they could give some sort of information about where exactly they were right now. Then Twilight noticed a street vendor struggling to tie barrels of cargo to his cart. A wayward barrel sprang loose and toppled the entire pile. "Let me help you with that!" The princess sprang into action, using her magic to catch the barrel in question. But the beast just growled at her to get away from his cart.

"Now, I know we need help, but be careful who you talk to," Twilight warned the others in a low whisper. "And try to blend in!"

But it was too late. Pinkie Pie was already bounding forward into the market square, screaming at the top of her lungs. *"CAN ANYPONY TAKE US TO THE QUEEN OF THE HIPPOS?!"* she shouted gleefully.

A gigantic blue monster with fishlike fins scoffed in disgust at Pinkie's lack of awareness for the rules. "You want somethin', you gotta give somethin'!" he grunted.

"Oh!" Pinkie giggled and proceeded to offer the beast a big hug, a mane comb with a few curly pink hairs woven through its teeth, and a picture of her sister Maud. When he refused all her offers, Pinkie Pie held out a little white ball. "How about this breath mint?!" Pinkie leveled with the stinky-breathed fish monster. "Seriously, buddy. Help me help you."

Twilight and the others watched, growing more nervous with each passing minute. This didn't seem like the sort of place a pony should go around teasing anycreature. Twilight darted to Pinkie's side and pulled her away from the growling creature. "You can't just take off! And you don't need to announce to every—"

"Relax, Twilight! I've totally got this." Pinkie smiled, waving her hoof nonchalantly. But the two pony friends were so caught up in their conversation that they didn't notice a group of the ruffians closing in on them! Rarity, Applejack, and Fluttershy took a few steps back toward one another. Even Rainbow Dash looked shaken by the shouts of the pushy mob.

"How much for the giant gecko?!" yelled one, pointing to Spike.

"Uh..." Twilight shook her head. "Spike isn't for sale—"

"I *want* that fancy purple hair!" shouted another. "I'll give you *two hippos* for it!"

"*Two* hippos?!" Rarity cried out indignantly. "It's worth more than *that*." Unfortunately, this only caused the bidding war for everything the ponies had—and the ponies themselves—to get louder. The vendors shouted and argued with one another over their pony prizes as they got closer and closer to the ponies.

The friends held on to one another in terror and closed their eyes. Twilight couldn't help but think that this could be the end of their journey, before it had even begun.

CHAPTER NINE

A mysterious fellow named Capper had been watching the entire fiasco from the shadows. The lanky golden-colored cat slunk around in his shabby deep-red duster coat. His shocking green eyes and the curl of purple fur on the top of his head made him stand out in a crowd—when he wanted to, that was. And luckily for the little ponies, he decided right now was the perfect time to do so.

"Back up, everyone!" Capper leaped into the middle of the crowd, landing gracefully on his hind legs right in front of the scared ponies. *"Back. It. Up!"* He extended his arms protectively to the greedy crowd of hooligans and spoke directly to them. "Y'all are in some serious danger! Now, you didn't touch any of them, did you?" He pointed to the ponies and feigned concern. It was enough to stop the vendors in their tracks.

"Just look at all those colors—you think that's natural?" Capper leaned in close and whispered, "They're infected with 'Pastelus Coloritis'!"

The crowd gasped in horror, even though they had no idea what that was. It just sounded quite serious.

Applejack couldn't abide the implication that she and her friends were sick. Why—they were healthy as horses! She stepped forward in a defensive huff. "Now, you listen here, fella—"

Capper shot her a look and covered Applejack's mouth with his tail. Then he slyly dipped his tail into some nearby purple liquid and flung it at the nearest creature. The giant fish man didn't notice. "Don't worry, though…" Capper waltzed and weaved through the crowd in a dizzying movement. "As long as you're not covered in purple splotches, you'll be *fine*." Capper gasped and pointed at the giant fish man's arms, where the splotches of purple liquid had landed. "Uh-oh…"

"What do I do?!" the fish man cried out in desperation. The other creatures started to slowly back away from him.

"Enjoy your last moments." Capper smirked. "And don't touch anyone—because parts *will* fall off."

"Aaaaaahhh!" the crowd screamed, completely forgetting about their pony and Dragon prey. Without a second thought, they scrambled to get as far away as possible. Clouds of dust were kicked up in the process, and when they settled a moment later, the only souls in the whole vicinity were Capper and the ponies.

"Well, all right…" The smug cat spun on his paws and turned back to his new friends to see just how impressed they were with his quick thinking. He grabbed the lapels of his red coat and raised his eyebrows expectantly.

"You. Are. *Awesome!*" Rainbow Dash flew over, her face breaking out into a look of pure admiration.

"And quite charming…" Rarity giggled and blushed, oblivious to Spike's jealous grunt.

"Capper's the name," said the cat with a wink. "And charming's my game." He bent down in a deep, formal bow. He locked eyes with Twilight Sparkle. "So, shall I lead you to the hippos, then?"

While Pinkie Pie and the others began to follow the cat out of the square, something inside was telling Twilight to be cautious. She held out her wing in front of Pinkie and hissed, "Wait! I don't know if we should trust him…."

"We could definitely use a friend out here!" Pinkie reminded her. But before Twilight could even consider Pinkie's point, Capper popped in between the two of them.

"You know what?" Capper said, voice as smooth as a purr. "Little Cotton-Candy Hair is right. This town is not a nice place for little fillies all alone."

"We're not alone," Twilight pointed out. She gestured to her friends. "We have each other."

Capper nodded. "Ah yes, but *I* know every nook and cranny, every dark twist and corner of this place! You're all actually quite lucky you ran into me...." His green eyes glowed with mischief.

Applejack cocked her head to the side. "So what're ya sayin', exactly?"

"I'll be the friend you need!" Capper smiled and tugged at his ragged coat. "Follow me, and I'll lead you to safety." The cat skipped ahead in a nimble fashion. "And help you find the hippos you seek!"

Finding the Queen of the Hippos was exactly what they needed, so Twilight nodded at the others to go. As they followed Capper, the ponies and Spike all looked to one another for reassurance. Everypony's face seemed a little unsure, except for Pinkie Pie's. But Capper was right—Klugetown was an unfamiliar place, and he *had* saved them from the villagers. What more proof did they need that he was on their side?

CHAPTER TEN

The ponies followed Capper, darting through the darkened streets, past creepy alleyways and tattered curtains in a labyrinthine spiral. Now and then, Capper would scurry ahead and whisper something to a random villager. Whatever he was saying allowed the group access through secret shortcuts, so the ponies didn't mind a little bit of clandestine activity.

Finally, they arrived at a gigantic water mill. Capper hopped onto the wheel and motioned for them to do the same. A moment later, they were whisked up into the belly of the mill tower.

"Welcome, my little ponies, to my little manor!" Capper announced with pride as they finally entered the funky dwelling. The ponies filed in, and Capper got busy at once, trying to make them feel comfortable. It wasn't difficult, because his cozy hideaway was chock-full with treasures of all kinds to explore, soft pillows to sit on, and refreshments to warm their bellies. It was just what they needed.

"How lovely," cooed Rarity, settling into a purple armchair. She noticed that her mane blended in to the color. It looked fabulous.

"Oh, I feel better already!" Fluttershy said with a satisfied sigh.

Capper pointed to Spike, looking slightly concerned. "Oh, uh, did you house-train this baby crocodile?"

"Crocodile?!" Spike repeated with a bitter grunt. The little Dragon might have been the only one in the group who was unimpressed by Capper. Spike even caught Rarity subtly mooning over an old painting with Capper's face in it.

"So this Queen of the Hippos—what kind of powers does she have?" Twilight trotted close behind Capper as he fumbled about, fluffing pillows and straightening up. "And how long will it take to get to her?"

"Hippos? Oh!" Capper was taken aback. He grabbed a stack of teacups and began to set the table. "Yeah, they got powers! Heavy, large powers...and, uh...I'll take you soon enough!"

Twilight's eye began to twitch. "We don't have time!"

"Please, please. Relax!" Capper insisted, holding out his paws. "Put your hooves up. There's always time for some dillydally tea." He poured a cup for Fluttershy, and she took a happy sip.

"Mmmm," she cooed. "This is wonderful."

"I guess we can stay for a few minutes...." Twilight bit her lip, feeling conflicted. It was nice to see her friends enjoy some rest and relief. The other ponies and Spike didn't *have* to come with her on this journey, and they deserved a few moments to regroup. Even Applejack and Rainbow Dash sipped their tea gratefully—and they didn't usually like tea!

But that didn't mean Twilight couldn't make good

use of this time to learn something from their gracious host. The very instant they'd entered Capper's manor, Twilight had noticed the various bookshelves lining the walls. She trotted over to one of them and scanned the titles. Twilight had no idea what she was looking for—a book on hippos? It seemed extremely unlikely that she would find such a perfect answer right in front of her face, but it was worth a shot.

A very old, ornate tome caught her eye. It was a deep-maroon color, with gilded edges and a mysterious map on the cover. It appeared to be an old atlas. Twilight used her magic to gently lift the book from the shelf. But as she did, a loose piece of paper fell out!

"Huh?" Twilight mumbled to herself as she unfolded the discovery. She couldn't contain a gasp as she laid her eyes on it. This was their key to finding the queen! The ponies had been looking for the wrong thing the entire time.

CHAPTER ELEVEN

Please!" a long-necked vendor cried out as a Storm Creature smashed her booth. "I don't know anything!"

The Storm Creatures tore across the main plaza of Klugetown with no regard for the destruction they were causing to the vendor booths. They had strict orders to do anything in their power to find the wretched purple princess pony who had escaped back in Canterlot. Villagers screamed and darted away, frightened by the growls and ferocity that punctuated the massive soldiers' movements.

Tempest Shadow trotted stoically behind them. This side trip was a mere inconvenience to her. All she had to do was find the princess and get back to Canterlot. It wouldn't be difficult. That Twilight Sparkle was weak—Tempest just knew it.

"You really think the ponies got this far?" Grubber asked, walking alongside his master and munching on an apple tart. He was constantly eating.

Tempest narrowed her eyes and stopped in her tracks. She noticed a bright-pink strand of pony hair caught in a jagged piece of wooden fence. "Oh, they're here." This confirmation was all she needed.

"Attention!" Tempest called out, her voice strong and even. "A little purple pony passed this way. Tell me where she is—"

"Or somethin' real bad's gonna happen!" Grubber added. The bite of apple tart he took right after really didn't do much to make him seem intimidating.

"You think we're gonna fall for this again?" The giant blue fish man who'd been told he had the dreaded "Pastelus Coloritis" stepped forward. Obviously, despite what he'd been told, the beast still had all his parts. He frowned. "I don't know what kinda scam you're working with Capper and the rest of your friends, but—"

Tempest cut him off. "Friends?" She had assumed the little purple pony was working alone.

"Poison or no poison…you're gonna pay!" The fish man came at Tempest, thrusting his fishy fist at her muzzle. She snapped into action, ducking his punch. Tempest shot into the air, grabbing the fin that had nearly caught her muzzle. Then she swung the massive beast down to the ground with a giant crash! The fish man groaned in pain.

"Now," the satisfied Unicorn said as she stood over him, her broken horn sparking and sputtering with electric energy, "about this 'Capper'…." From the terrified look on the face of the not-so-formidable fish monster, Tempest Shadow knew she was going to get all the information she needed.

CHAPTER TWELVE

The ponies were all gathered around Capper, sharing stories from Equestria. Rainbow Dash was deep into her story about the first time she'd ever successfully performed a Sonic Rainboom—the most epic stunt a Pegasus could attempt—when Rarity trotted over to fix Capper's coat. She'd found some spare thread and a few buttons, and she used her magic to make a few quick, expert stitches.

"Here you go!" Rarity declared as she finished up. "I do apologize. If we were back home, I could have matched the coat from your portrait." The Unicorn gestured her hoof to the painting on the wall.

"Whoa." Capper's jaw dropped when he caught

his reflection in the mirror. He couldn't believe how much better his coat looked. It was almost like new! But why was Rarity helping him with this? Capper stroked his whiskers and raised his eyebrow. "Okay, what's the catch?"

"Nothing! After all you've done for us?" Rarity smiled warmly. "Consider it a thank-you."

"Oh, don't thank me. Really..." A wave of guilt washed over Capper. What had he done to these poor ponies, who now considered him a friend? He deflated with the weight of his secret. Capper opened his mouth, considering telling them the truth as to why he was being so hospitable, when Twilight Sparkle came rushing into the room.

"We've been looking for the wrong queen!" Twilight exclaimed. She unfurled a scroll and laid it on the table. It was a map! The ponies all gathered around to look. Twilight pointed her hoof at an illustration. "We don't need the Queen of the Hippos—we need the Queen of the *Hippogriffs*! Part pony, part eagle."

The ponies all turned to Capper for insight on the

development. It didn't really add up. Capper scrambled to come up with something. "Oh! The Hippo-*griffs*? Now, the trouble with that is, no one knows where they are...."

Twilight frowned suspiciously. "It says right here they're on top of Mount Aris."

"*Oooh!*" Pinkie Pie pointed her hoof at the window. "You mean the mountain right outside?" Sure enough, far off in the distance was a tall peak surrounded by clouds that looked almost identical to the one in the map's illustration.

Twilight couldn't believe Capper had withheld such important information from them, when he'd clearly known about the Hippogriffs all along. She shot him a disappointed look, folded her map, and turned to her friends. "Let's go, everypony."

"Wait!" The cat sprang to the doorway in a panic, blocking the ponies' way. "You can't make it there by yourselves! You need an airship—and lucky for you, I can get you a ride!"

Twilight narrowed her eyes and pushed past him. "I think we can get there on our own...."

But when she opened the door, a big naked mole rat (thankfully not *literally* naked in his raggedy suit and top hat) stood waiting outside! He smiled, exposing his sickly yellow teeth. "Here's Verko!" He laughed with a sneaky satisfaction. He leaned past Twilight and met Capper's eyes. "These ponies better shoot rainbow lasers outta their eyes if they're going to settle your debt, Capper!" He gestured to a gigantic cage on wheels behind him. "Let's load 'em up!"

The ponies gasped in horror. Capper was going to *sell them*?! Applejack shook her head in disappointment, and Rarity had to fan herself with her hoof to get over the shock of it all. What a double-crossing, good-for-nothing feline scoundrel! All Capper did in reply was tug on his coat collar and laugh nervously. That confirmed his guilt.

Verko scampered in, his naked mole rat feet scratching against the floor. He had just begun to size up the ponies when a faint sparking sound came from outside. *Clip, clop. Clip, clop.* The sound of hooves followed, and a shadowy figure appeared in the outline of the doorway. "Silly little ponies..."

"Tempest!" Twilight gasped. Her worst fears were starting to come true! She and her friends were going to be captured, and they would never be able to save Equestria. Everypony was visibly shaken. Fluttershy cowered behind the others in fear.

"Trusting strangers, I see?" Tempest Shadow motioned at Capper and trotted in, raising a confident brow. "Big mistake. *Big.*"

"Huge!" Grubber added, following his master.

Verko, the salesmole, scrambled over to the new guests. Maybe he could make a quick bit off this strange pony, too! He took Tempest's cheeks in his claws and squashed them around. "Scary broken horn! What tricks do you know, my little pony-wony?"

Tempest's horn sparked menacingly.

Suddenly, she sent a shock of lightning at Verko!

It was now or never. Twilight and her friends had to make good use of this moment of chaos.

"Go, go!" Twilight whispered as she opened the window with her magic. The ponies sprang into action. They were all out the window, map in tow, before Verko even hit the floor from Tempest's stunning blast.

When Tempest saw Twilight fly out the window, she began to sizzle with rage. "Get her—now!" she called out to her Storm Guard, stomping her hoof on the ground.

Tempest didn't understand what was happening. How could that little princess have escaped her grasp a second time?! Tempest had underestimated the purple pony, but one thing was for sure: Twilight Sparkle wouldn't escape again. Tempest Shadow and the Storm King would make sure of that.

+ CHAPTER THIRTEEN + +

*A*aaaaahhh!" the ponies screamed as they barreled through Klugetown. Who could have predicted that the giant wooden water-mill wheel would come loose when they all jumped on it outside Capper's manor? They clutched tightly to the wheel's surface as Rainbow Dash and Twilight tried to steer the makeshift craft out of harm's way. It was no use!

The Storm Guard was hot on their hooves as the mill wheel rolled through streets and buildings, shattering everything in its path. Somepony had to stop this thing. "Jump!" Applejack cried out as soon as she spotted a jagged elevated walkway. The ponies leaped to the wooden planks and galloped across, the wheel now careening toward them!

"We have to get there!" Twilight Sparkle shouted, and pointed her hoof directly ahead of them. "To the docks!" Several walkways jutted out from the side of a tall building. Anchored to the highest port was one massive floating ship! It definitely wasn't one of the Storm King's fleet.

But it *was* in the process of leaving!

"Hurry!" Twilight urged as she soared behind her friends to make sure they were all safe. The ponies' manes billowed behind them as they galloped as fast as their hooves would carry them to the airship.

Rainbow Dash, in a moment of quick thinking, flew ahead and grabbed the mooring rope with her teeth. She pulled it taut enough for Rarity, Applejack, and Spike to carefully tightrope across.

Fluttershy flew above, spotting and encouraging them. "That's it! Don't look down now."

"YAY!" squealed Pinkie Pie as she took an enthusiastic

leap onto the rope. The weight caused the rope to buckle. Spike began to lose his footing, and disaster struck. Spike and most of the ponies managed to grab hold of the rope, but Pinkie Pie wasn't so lucky. The pink pony wailed in despair as she plummeted down, heading right in the direction of some very craggy-looking rocks!

"Pinkie!" Twilight cried out as she darted to the other pony's rescue. She reached her friend with just a second to spare and carried her back up to safety on the deck of the ship with the others.

Almost immediately, Pinkie popped up and excitedly thrust her hoof into the air. "Best. Escape plan. *Ever!*" Twilight started to protest, but suddenly she and Pinkie found themselves lassoed and dragged away.

Applejack had pulled them behind a wall of cargo. *"Shhhh!"*

"Hey, did you hear somethin'?" one big shadowy figure said to his buddy, who just squawked in reply. From their outlines, they looked like large... birds? Perhaps they were Griffon sailors! Twilight felt a twinge of hope. She knew the Griffon Kingdom—maybe these Griffon strangers would know some of her friends and help deliver her to Mount Aris as an act of goodwill and friendship to Equestria. What a stroke of luck landing on this ship had been!

They were already heading in the right direction. It should be no problem finding the Queen of the Hippogriffs. After they got her help, all this would be over soon. Twilight could just feel it.

"Okay!" Capper wailed as the Storm Creatures threw him onto the dock by Tempest's airship. Being taken prisoner by the Storm Guard was not something that had been in his plans today. "No need for violence! The ponies are headed to..." Capper almost told the truth and hesitated, thinking of how the kind ponies had mended his coat and called him "friend." They didn't deserve to be given up so easily again.

Tempest Shadow bore over him, tapping her hoof impatiently. "Well?"

"They're headed east! Yeah…to Black Skull Island." Capper nodded with his signature cool-cat confidence. "So glad I could be of service! I'll just be on my way—"

Tempest stepped in front of Capper, blocking his path. "When I get my princess. Until then, your fate is still…up in the air." Capper's face fell. This couldn't be happening.

"*Ohhhh!* You're gonna go in a skiff!" Grubber laughed in delight. "Which is a boat—specifically, an airboat." The squat creature motioned to the warriors. Once their captive was tied up and safe inside, Tempest took the helm. Time was running out before the Storm King's arrival.

And Tempest could not afford to fail him.

CHAPTER FOURTEEN

As the airship soared through the misty clouds, Twilight studied the map she'd taken from Capper's place. Judging by the landmarks in the illustration, Twilight was fairly confident they were heading in the direction of Mount Aris, but they needed to be sure. There was only one way to find out where this ship was actually going. They would have to talk to somecreature.

Applejack and Rainbow Dash peered out from behind a wooden crate to assess their situation. The crew members of the airship kind of looked like giant birds—but they definitely weren't Griffons. They wore

black uniforms and grumpy expressions as they wad-
dled back and forth across the deck with their boxes of
mysterious cargo.

"What do ya think, Twilight?" Applejack asked.
"Should we just...ask 'em to take us?"

Twilight bit her lip, unsure. "The last time we
trusted someone, he tried to sell us!" The other ponies
nodded, considering this. None of them could quite
believe they'd almost been caged and sold as goods.

Suddenly, their hiding place started to shift. A box
was lifted, and the ponies were seen! Staring straight
back at them was a gigantic green parrot with a scowl
on his face. "Hey, Captain Celaeno!" shouted one of
the birds. "We supposed to be shipping livestock today?"

A white-feathered bird with a crystal peg leg hob-
bled forward and sighed. "No, Boyle...looks like we
have stowaways." She appeared to be more inconve-
nienced by the discovery than upset. Boyle and Captain Celaeno looked to each other for an answer,
but they both came up short. The latter whipped out

a huge book and began to leaf through it. She had clearly been through this routine before.

"The Storm King's rule book says…" Captain Celaeno read, then paused. She turned to the rest of her parrot crew and shouted, *"Throw 'em overboard!"*

Overboard? Twilight and her friends huddled together as they braced themselves to be seized. Fluttershy kept her eyes shut and whimpered in fear as the parrots closed in. With each step closer, the ponies felt more hopeless. They were doomed. . . .

FWEEEEEE! At the sound of the whistle, every crew member stopped what they were doing and began to trudge away. "All right, that's lunch!" Captain Celaeno sighed. "C'mon, everybody; we get fifteen minutes! Scarf it down."

At the mere mention of food, Rainbow Dash's tummy began to rumble. It had been forever since the ponies last ate a meal, and as they were apparently not getting thrown overboard, she saw an opportunity. "Uh…can *we* have some food?"

"Food...food..." Captain Celaeno consulted her rule book. She slammed it shut and shrugged. "Eh, nothing here says you can't." The ponies cheered with excitement. Their fate had changed so quickly!

"Oh, thank goodness!" said Rarity, sighing with relief and silently wondering if the parrots usually had tea to go with the lunch. How delightful this was going to be!

But once seated at the long table on the mess deck, the ponies were presented with big slops of gruel. No sandwiches, no fresh apples, and certainly not a single drop of tea! "Oh, what a shame." Rarity laughed uncomfortably, sizing up her hefty portion of gruel. "I just ate...several days ago!"

The birds calmly chomped down on their chow, seemingly having forgotten all about the stowaway thing. Everycreature was distracted. Actually, there was something off about the whole ship. As if it used to be meant for something else.

"So you were about to toss us overboard..." Rainbow Dash said through a hefty mouthful of gruel. She ignored the panicked look from Twilight. "And you stopped for a lunch break?!"

Boyle, the green parrot who had discovered the ponies, put down his fork and slumped sadly. "The Storm King only allows us one break a day for meals. Then it's back to hauling goods."

Spike perked up. "So you're just delivery guys?"

"And gals," Captain Celaeno said, tugging on her unflattering uniform emblazoned with the Storm King's insignia. "These aren't exactly doing us any favors."

This is perfect, Twilight realized. If they were delivery birds, then they certainly could help out. What difference were a few little ponies instead of some cargo in the grand scheme of things? "Then, can you *deliver* us to Mount Aris?" she asked with a friendly smile.

"Sorry." Captain Celaeno shook her head. "We do what the Storm King orders. Or we suffer his wrath." She went back to eating her food and hating her life.

A moment of silence passed. "But what did you guys do *before* the Storm King?" Rainbow Dash pried.

She knew there was more to this story, and she wasn't giving up that easily. "What's that?" She pointed her hoof at a black flag that had been covered up by a poster of the Storm King.

Mullet, the first-mate bird, pulled the poster back. Underneath was a flag bearing the symbol of the skull and crossbones! Rainbow Dash gasped. She knew what that meant. "Whoa! You used to be *pirates*?!"

Princess Twilight Sparkle is so excited to help plan the Friendship Festival that's being held in Canterlot.

She might be taking things a little too seriously, though.

One of her best friends, Pinkie Pie, definitely agrees.

Applejack and Rarity are also helping make the festival the best it can be.

Just as Fluttershy is starting to get her groove on...

...a terrifying newcomer arrives, intent on stealing all the magic from the princesses of Equestria.

It's Tempest Shadow, with her henchman, Grubber,
and a whole battalion of Storm Creatures!

They're working for the mysterious Storm King,
who has plans to take over all Equestria.

Luckily for Twilight (and all Equestria), she and her friends are able to escape the attack and go on a quest to a place beyond Equestria to find somecreature who can help save the princesses.

Capper the cat is willing to help them...
but Tempest is never far behind.

The brave ponies—and Spike the Dragon—even meet some former pirates, and inspire them through the magic of song to return to their adventurous ways.

They're soon on the run again, however...this time headed for the mysterious Mount Aris. They are hopeful, but things are still pretty bleak for the group of friends.

After reaching their destination and finding it abandoned, the ponies dive deep underwater while chasing a mysterious light. Eventually, they meet Princess Skystar, a cheerful but lonely Seapony.

Transformed into Seaponies by a magic pearl, the ponies throw a signature Pinkie Pie party and have a really awesome time under the sea...

...until Twilight makes a bad decision that could ruin everything. And Tempest Shadow pounces on the opportunity!

Can Princess Twilight Sparkle, Applejack, Rarity, Fluttershy, Rainbow Dash, Pinkie Pie, and Spike save Equestria from the Storm King and his army?

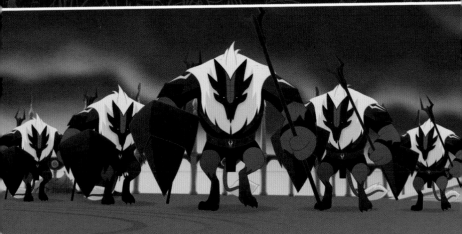

CHAPTER FIFTEEN

The birds looked at one another sheepishly. "We prefer the term *swashbuckling treasure hunters*," Mullet said with a sly smirk. He looked off into the distance, as though he was remembering his swashbuckling days gone by.

"So...pirates." Rainbow Dash smiled in satisfaction. She sprang to her hooves and looked Captain Celaeno in her sad eyes. "The way I see it—you birds have a choice to make."

"We do?" The birds were intrigued.

"What do you mean?" Boyle grunted.

Rainbow Dash flew over to the poster and gestured to it. "You can let some hoity-toity Storm King tell you how to live your lives or"—she ripped down the poster, letting the pirate flag fly free—"you can be *awesome* again!"

A murmur of whispers broke out among the bird shipmates. At first, Twilight was nervous that Rainbow Dash had offended their unlikely hosts, but it was quite the opposite. For the first time since the ponies had arrived on Captain Celaeno's ship, the birds were smiling!

"The rainbow pony is right," Captain Celaeno agreed as she stood up. "It's time to be awesome!" She puffed her chest out with pride. "Come on, scalawags! Let's show these little ponies how it's done!" The parrots cheered and followed orders, marching out to the top deck with their leader.

"*Yeahhh!*" Pinkie Pie cheered, bounding after them. The other ponies trotted out, grinning from ear to ear.

The birds got right to work restoring their ship to its former swashbuckling glory. They all sang and whistled as decks were swabbed, flags were flown, and chests of gems were unlocked and admired.

Back at the helm of her ship, Captain Celaeno placed

a huge pirate hat with a pink plume on her head. She stood proudly, a mischievous smile on her beak. The clouds opened up to bluer skies as Celaeno steered the airship. "This is the life!"

"Awesome!" Rainbow Dash cheered, zipping and zooming underneath the sails and past the pirate crew. "And now for the finishing touch!"

"Rainboom, Rainboom, Rainboom!" Pinkie Pie started the chant. It wasn't long before the other ponies and birds started chanting and clapping along in encouragement, too.

All except Twilight, who suddenly realized the implications of a gigantic signal showing their where-abouts. "Nonononono...*no!*" she cried out.

But it was too late. Rainbow Dash was already soaring into the sky with a huge smile on her face. Once she was far enough away, Rainbow Dash looped around and dove down at top speed. The Peg-asus looped again around the airship, creating a rain-bow spiral around the pirates. Everycreature watched in delighted wonder as the colorful pattern burst from every direction in a beautiful explosion. Captain Celaeno and her crew had never seen anything so spectacular before.

"Aw, yeah!" Rainbow Dash laughed. There was nothing more exhilarating than performing a Sonic Rainboom, especially after being cooped up for so long. *"Woooo!"* she shouted with unfettered glee.

Across the sky, Tempest Shadow also experienced something akin to happiness. Because the pretty picture in the sky was as good as a map for finding those little ponies.

"Change course from Black Skull Island to"— Tempest narrowed her eyes at Capper and pointed in the direction of the rainbow blast—*"that* way."

Grubber put down his piece of cake, nodded, and motioned to the beasts. It was too slow for her. She pushed him aside and spun the steering wheel herself. The entire ship lurched, and Tempest snickered. She hoped the ponies were having a good time, because it would be their last.

CHAPTER SIXTEEN

When the dark clouds began to roll in, Captain Celaeno knew. She sounded the alarm immediately. What was happening? Rainbow Dash and the other ponies looked to their new comrades for answers.

"Storm Guards!" Captain Celaeno squawked. "Looks like they found you!"

Twilight's face contorted into anguish. "Tempest!"

"Secure the rigging!" Captain Celaeno ordered. "Everyone—prepare for lockdown!"

Applejack's eyes were as wide as dinner plates. "Oh no!"

"Goodness!" Fluttershy whispered.

Boyle led Applejack, Pinkie Pie, Fluttershy, Rarity,

Rainbow Dash, and Spike to a trapdoor. They galloped inside to hide. Luckily, the transfixed Twilight slipped in at the very last moment. As the hatch shut, the ponies held their breaths and looked at one another.

Rainbow Dash finally broke the silence. "You... think she saw my Rainboom?" Her cheeks blushed pink with embarrassment. She had just been trying to liven up the party, not ruin their whole adventure!

"Are you *kidding* me?!" Twilight retorted. She began to pace around the room, which was never a good sign. "This is bad. This is bad. This is very, *very* bad!"

Suddenly, the airship lurched as a harpoon above deck made contact and began to reel them in to the skiff. *"Ahhh!"* the ponies shouted as they all fell into a pile. They craned their necks to listen as Tempest Shadow and the Storm Creatures boarded the craft. A long series of murmurs followed.

"What are they saying?!" Pinkie Pie whispered. "Nice things?"

"They're asking where *I* am!" Twilight exclaimed. She was already a ball of nerves. "Tempest is accusing them of sheltering fugitives and threatening them with the wrath of the Storm King...." Twilight began to panic. "We have to get off this ship before they tell Tempest we're here!"

Rainbow Dash scoffed. "We helped them get their mojo back. They're not going to give us up!" Rarity and Applejack nodded in agreement, but it did nothing to calm Twilight. She was getting that twitchy look she sometimes had when she was trying to impress the other princesses. But all they could do was keep quiet and wait it out.

Up above, Tempest had had enough. She'd pointed out Captain Celaeno and her crew's silly outfits. They were supposed to be wearing standard-issue Storm King–brand delivery gear. Celaeno claimed they were having a pirate-themed party. It was very fishy. The rule book didn't allow time for parties, so they were definitely lying.

"You know who else is really good at parties?" Tempest growled. "*Ponies.* Now, I'm gonna count to three, and if you don't tell me where they are, your ship is going down!" But before she could even count, Tempest was interrupted by a loud shriek. She galloped over to the underbelly. One glance confirmed it—the ponies had escaped through the trapdoor in the bottom of the airship.

"What?!" Tempest's shrill voice rang out. She scanned the sky for the colorful equines but couldn't find anything. Tempest stomped her hoof on the deck in frustration. She peered over the edge one last time, hoping the ponies had all made it out alive. Not because she cared much, but because Tempest wanted that princess in one piece. And she would get her.

"Hey, Tempest!" Grubber shouted. He ambled up, holding a cupcake and a worn piece of scroll.

"What's that?!" she barked. Couldn't he see she was busy trying to wallow in her own frustration right now?

"I found this. It's a kind of cupcake thing with sprinkles...." Grubber grinned. "And this is...uh..."

Tempest yanked the scroll from his claw and unfurled it. There were crazy-looking scribbles all over it. "It's a map," Tempest observed. And it was the perfect clue. "They're going to Mount Aris."

CHAPTER SEVENTEEN

*H*eeyew!" Applejack sighed with relief. She placed her hooves on the edge of the wooden box that had become their makeshift hot-air balloon basket and peered out at the landscape of bushy green trees below. "That was some quick thinkin', Twilight!"

"Yes, darling!" Rarity marveled. "How in the world did you gather all those items and assemble them in midair while we were plummeting to our own doom?" She smoothed down her mane. "And using Spike's fire-breathing abilities to heat the balloon? Truly inspired." Spike beamed at the compliment.

"Next stop, Mount Aris!" Rainbow Dash called out

as she flew alongside the hot-air balloon. She pointed to the narrow, pointy mountain in the distance.

"I don't know how I did it," Twilight admitted. "But it was great. And now we're home free!" She took a deep breath. The air somehow seemed sweeter on the heels of victory. *"Yahooo!"*

The stone stairs to Mount Aris were winding and endless. As they trudged upward, the ponies were reaching a new level of exhaustion. It didn't help that the landscape was completely desolate, either. It was pretty depressing.

Rarity, in particular, was beginning to get quite whiny. "That's it! I simply. Cannot. Even! I have nothing. The bad guys have won!" She collapsed into a dramatic heap on the ground. "I'm so sorry...."

Rainbow Dash, who had been periodically flying above to check their progress, called down some words of encouragement. "We're almost there!"

"Will you stop saying that?" Rarity huffed. Instances such as these were the only times she was truly jealous of Rainbow Dash for having wings.

Rainbow brightened. "No, really—we're here!"

It was the final push they all needed. The ponies sped up, taking the last sets of stairs twice as fast. When they reached the top and saw the entrance, it all felt worth the journey. "This is it!" Twilight exclaimed. Excitement bubbled up inside her stomach.

They all stood back and admired the sight. The gates of Mount Aris—home of the Hippogriffs—were quite eerie and beautiful. Two ancient stone columns carved into Hippogriffs flanked the walkway, inviting visitors in with a sense of mystery and mysticism. Twilight, a history buff, felt a twinge of intrigue that made her want to read everything ever written about these creatures. She could recall learning next to nothing about them in her studies.

"Well, I'll be!" marveled Applejack, leaning back so far that her brown hat almost fell clean off her noggin.

Once she'd secured it back on her head, she trotted in through the gates behind the others.

"Are we sure this is the right place?" asked Rarity, looking around the deserted stone street. It did look a little worse for wear with all the cracked statues and toppled pillars everywhere. Many of the doors to the beautiful, dome-shaped dwellings had been left ajar, and weeds had begun to grow everywhere.

"Hello?" Applejack called out. "Is anypony home?"

Pinkie Pie took a different approach. She bounced around, looking for any signs of life. "No Hippogriffies here. Or here. Or here! Wait..." Pinkie crouched down and lifted a little rock with her muzzle. "Nope. This place is emp-ty!"

Empty? After everything the ponies had gone through to get here, Twilight didn't understand how this was possible. Celestia *had* to believe that the only way to save Equestria was to find the Queen of the Hippogriffs, or she wouldn't have instructed Luna to go find her. Plus, the map Twilight had found at

Capper's had led them right here. None of it made any sense.

"Well, where are they?" Twilight said in disbelief.

Spike scanned the desolate landscape and shuddered. "Something bad happened here. Something turned this whole place into a ghost town!"

"A gh-gh-ghost town?" Fluttershy whimpered. She didn't like the idea of ghosts or anything remotely scary.

"Wait!" Rarity perked up and began to look around. "What's that gorgeous sound? It's like a song...." The ponies listened closely.

There *was* a beautiful voice echoing through the empty city. *"Aaaaaah...ahhhhh...ahhhhh!"* The melody was familiar and haunting at the same time. The ponies bravely trotted along, searching for the source.

"It's coming from over there!" In the distance, Twilight noticed an interesting building with tall archways. Like everything else in the area, it had been partially destroyed, but it looked as if it were once a magnificent castle.

Once the ponies were inside, the singing grew louder. The sound was amplified by the acoustics of the cavernous space. *"Ahhhh...ahhhh..."* The pretty melody continued, but it was now accompanied by the splish-splash of running water, for there was a large fountain in the center of the room. It was set in the middle of a small pond and shaped like a pink lotus flower, just like the kind the ponies used in treatments back at the La Ti Da Spa back in Ponyville.

Was that a shadow of somepony behind the flower? It was too murky to see the fountain properly. Rarity stepped forward for a closer look and marveled at its sheer beauty. A few rocks under her hoof tumbled down and plopped into the water.

"What was that?!"

The shadowy figure gasped and leaped into the water, causing a splash to spray onto the ponies.

Twilight and Rarity exchanged an excited look. The Hippogriffs may have been long gone from this place, but there was definitely somecreature here. Maybe this mystery creature could help them find the queen! It wasn't much, but a droplet of hope was better than nothing.

"Hey! Wait up!" Pinkie Pie called out to the creature. She leaped without hesitation into the water. *"CANNONBALL!"*

"Pinkie!" Twilight cried out, and jumped in after her. One by one, the other ponies and Spike jumped in, too. *SPLASH!* But the creature was gone. Pinkie's mane dripped, sad and wet, against her face.

Applejack was about to console her friend when the pond started to swirl, pulling them into a whirlpool! "What in the hay?!"

"AAAAAHHH!" they all screamed in unison.

The ponies were being sucked underwater, and there was no way to escape.

+ + CHAPTER EIGHTEEN + +

Everything was dark. Twilight moved her hooves around, reaching for anything to grab on to, but all she felt was the sensation of being submerged in deep water. She was still holding her breath and desperately needed air. Twilight wanted to magically procure some, but everything felt fuzzy, and she couldn't remember how to use her horn until...

POP! A bubble appeared around Twilight's head. She exhaled gratefully and lit up her horn. All her friends were wearing head bubbles, too! They looked just as relieved as she did.

"Way to leave it till the last minute, Twilight!" Pinkie Pie joked, tapping her hoof on the sturdy surface.

Twilight shook her head, incredulous. "I didn't make these bubbles...."

"Then..." Fluttershy's eyes grew wide with a mixture of fear and wonder. "Who did?" She swam closer to the other ponies, and they formed a little underwater huddle.

Suddenly, something swam past! It was impossible to tell what, but it looked like the dark outline of a fish. Twilight really hoped it wasn't a shark. "Hello?" she called out. "We're looking for the Hippogriffs."

A glowing yellow orb shot toward the ponies, lighting up the whole area. It was so bright and mesmerizing. "How do I know I can trust you?" it asked.

"Please!" Twilight Sparkle begged. "The Storm King invaded our land, and we need to find the Hippogriffs—"

"The Storm King?!" The orb glowed even brighter as it came closer, transforming into something incredible. Twilight had never thought they were real, but swimming right before them was definitely a Seapony! Her face and front hooves were similar to a regular pony's, but she had pale-yellow scales, aqua-colored fins instead of a mane, pink fluttery wings, and a beautiful fish's tail instead of back hooves. She introduced herself as Princess Skystar.

"I'm so glad I saved you guys!" she squealed in a cute voice. She sounded even more chipper than Pinkie Pie did after eating cupcakes. "I'm totally taking you guys to my mom!"

Princess Skystar grabbed Twilight's hoof. The ponies formed a chain and let her lead them down into the watery unknown. They swam past rocks and schools of colorful fish, into a sea cave tunnel, and beyond. "We're almost there!" Skystar assured them. She giggled in excited anticipation as she swam through a rocky opening and into a glowing underwater paradise.

"This is where I live!" Skystar held out her hoof to present the view to the ponies with pride. Happy Seapony families swam around a sparkling wonderland, giving their princess a little nod as she passed by and clearly wondering about the curious strangers she was escorting. Just up ahead, a palace in the shape of an upside-down flower opened to receive Skystar and her guests.

"Wow!" Spike marveled, unable to control the direction of his floating. Rainbow Dash helped to spin him upright again.

"I know! I know!" Skystar giggled happily. Her visitors had barely seen anything yet, and they were already impressed. Once they'd swum up into the flower palace, Skystar approached a pearly-white Seapony with purple fins lounging luxuriously on a purple throne. She wore a golden crown. Skystar swam up to her. "Mother! Look what I found!"

"Is it another shell?" the queen replied without looking up. "Because I am telling you, if it is another shell, I am—" When she finally did notice Twilight and the others, she let out a massive gasp. "Princess Skystar! What have you done?! You know surface dwellers are forbidden here!" At this, several royal guards sprang into action, surrounding the ponies with spears.

"Nononono, MomMomMomMom, *please*!" Princess

Skystar whined. "It is *so* not like that! The Storm King is trying to destroy their home, too."

"We need to find the Hippogriffs," Twilight called out bravely. The guard pointing a spear at her narrowed his eyes, but Twilight ignored him. This was important. "Do you know what happened to them?"

The royal Seapony sighed. "Well, of course I know. I'm the queen. I know *everything*."

"Oooh! Oooh!" Princess Skystar smiled widely and clasped her finned hooves together in unabashed delight. "It is such a good story!"

But the queen held back for some reason. "Don't you dare tell them!" she chided her daughter, and the two began to playfully bicker. Ultimately, Skystar ignored her mother's wishes and swam up to the wall of the palace.

"Once upon a time, like…a while ago, the Hippogriffs *did* live on Mount Aris!" Skystar touched the wall with her hoof, and it began to light up magically with a glowing illustration of the Hippogriffs and the

Storm King. "But that horned beast showed up to steal their magic!"

Twilight met the worried eyes of Applejack and Rainbow Dash. They were all nervous to hear the next part. Spike was biting his lip. What if Skystar said the Storm King had eradicated the Hippogriffs entirely? What would that mean for Equestria? The bubbles on their heads allowed them to breathe, but they all held their breaths in nervous anticipation.

"But"—Skystar smiled brightly—"to keep their kingdom out his clutches, their brave and majestic leader, Queen Novo, hid them deep underwater, where he could never go." The wall glowed with a scene depicting the same beautiful Seapony kingdom in which they were now floating! "We *are*...well, we *were*...the Hippogriffs!" Skystar gestured to the palace and the Seaponies around them. She let out a jovial giggle. *"TA-DAH!"*

"Well, I guess the pearl is out of the oyster now." The older Seapony sighed. *"I* am the Queen of the Hippogriffs."

Twilight found herself grinning with delight. They had really found her—the Queen of the Hippogriffs was right in front of them! She didn't seem overly accommodating, but Skystar seemed to really like Twilight and her friends. She would definitely help save Equestria!

"Hold on; now, let me get this straight." Applejack cocked her head to the side. "When the Storm King came, you just abandoned your entire city and fled?"

Skystar smiled and rolled her eyes. "We didn't flee! We *swam....* You know, in order to flee!"

"But how?" asked Rainbow Dash. Ponies didn't randomly transform into other species, so she couldn't imagine how the Hippogriffs had managed it.

"Oh!" Princess Skystar swam over to her mother. She began to flip her tail and twirl around. "Can we show them? These are the first guests we've had in, like, *forever*! *Canwe canwe canwe canwe canwe canwe?!*"

Queen Novo raised an eyebrow and sized up the ponies again, still considering if it was a good idea that they were there. It seemed like she had come to the conclusion that the damage had been done. "Well, I suppose I should make, sure it still works," she said, swimming up to the giant jellyfish above her throne. Queen Novo gave it a gentle tap, and immediately, the tendrils parted to reveal a glittering, luminescent pearl.

It glowed so brightly that its light touched the entire palace. Magic began to swirl around, reaching for Spike and the ponies. Before they could even realize what was happening, they were transformed into Seaponies as well!

"These fins are divine!" gushed Rarity, admiring her pretty new fish's tail. The purple fins were curled perfectly, just as her tail had been.

Rainbow Dash sped around in a circle with expert form. Swimming was entirely different from flying, but she could tell it was just as awesome. She zoomed back to her friends. "Hey, Applejack! I'll race you to that coral!"

"You're on!" Applejack called back, and the two of them zipped away.

"Woo-hoo!" Pinkie Pie laughed, doing twirls and blowing bubbles. "Try it, Fluttershy!"

"Yay," Fluttershy said softly. She barely moved her tail.

"Guys," Spike said in confusion. "Guys! What is happening?!" The poor Dragon had become a puffer fish! He ballooned out and began to float up. Everypony giggled.

Twilight observed her friends with elation. She swam up to Novo and Skystar and said, "This is amazing! With this, we could transform everypony at home into something *powerful* enough to face the Storm King's army!"

Queen Novo's face grew dark. "Or it could end up in his greedy claws." She swam back to her beloved treasure and plucked it away. Novo clearly didn't like how sad it made the young purple pony to see her take it back to the jellyfish, but her jaw was set— she also clearly knew what she had to do. "Honey, I'm sorry about your home. I truly am. But my responsibility is to protect *my* subjects. The pearl is not going anywhere."

But they had come all this way. Queen Novo and the Seaponies couldn't just hide down here forever. There was so much they were missing up on land! As the queen bid the group farewell and left for her afternoon seaweed wrap, Twilight could keep only one thing on her mind—that pearl. She was going to borrow it. Hopefully, before anypony found out.

CHAPTER NINETEEN

Princess Skystar was quite apologetic about her mother's behavior. She explained that it had been such a long time since her mother, or any Seapony for that matter, had interacted with outsiders. They had grown wary of anypony who wasn't with them, because they might be against them. And even though their ordeal with the Storm King had been a long time ago, they were still very afraid of his wrath.

"So that's it," said Applejack, feeling defeated. "You can't help us? We left home for nothin'?"

"No..." Princess Skystar brightened. "Omigosh, I have the best idea—you can stay with us...*forever!*"

She swam back and forth, her pretty aqua fins shaking with excited fervor. "There are so many things we can do! We could make friendship bracelets out of shells, and picture frames out of shells, and decorative wastebaskets out of shells. Oh, it's so wonderful to have new friends to share my shells with!"

"Oh, oh..." Rarity said gently. She hated to shoot down the hopeful look in Skystar's eyes after she had been so wonderful to them. "That sounds lovely, darling, but you must realize we can't stay."

The Seapony princess slumped in sadness. "Oh, no. Of course. Of course! Of course you have your own friends back home. It's fine—it's fine!" She turned around to go, completely deflated. "It's probably for the best. Yeah, I'll just, um, I'll get Mom to, uh, turn you back so you can go home."

Pinkie Pie felt just awful. The thing that she hated more than anything in world—or the sea—was seeing somepony be so gloomy. "I *know* we have to go, but you guys saw how disappointed Princess Skystar was. Couldn't we stay for just a little longer?"

Applejack was about to protest, when Twilight surprised everypony. "Pinkie's right," Twilight said with a nod. "We do have time to do one small thing with Skystar!" Twilight's eyes darted around.

"Say what, now?" Rainbow Dash asked, suspicious.

"Well, we still need to come up with a plan to get back. A few minutes won't make a huge difference. And if there's anypony who can cram a lifetime of fun into a blink of an eye, it's Pinkie Pie. So go ahead and show Skystar the best time ever!" Twilight chirped. She threw up her finned hooves and gestured for them all to go. "I'll catch up with you."

Once they'd swum off to entertain Princess Skystar, Twilight was finally alone with the jellyfish. She scanned the room to make sure she was truly by herself. Luckily, the Seapony guards had followed Queen Novo to her appointments. It was Twilight's chance to do something sneaky. She was going to steal the Seaponies' pearl!

"Come on," Twilight said softly to herself, and

approached the jellyfish just as Queen Novo had. She reached out her finned hoof and gently tapped on one of the tentacles. Instead of parting to reveal the pearl for taking, the tentacles reached for Twilight and curled around her hooves! She was trapped. The more she struggled against their grasp, the tighter they wound around her. *"Ahhh!"* Twilight screamed. She hadn't meant to cause a commotion, but it was too late.

Within seconds, the Seapony guards returned to find the thief tangled in the scene. They looked furious, but not as angry as Queen Novo, who swam up after them. "All this so you could sneak in and take the pearl? See, Skystar? This is why we don't bring strangers to our home!"

Applejack, Rainbow Dash, Rarity, Pinkie Pie, Fluttershy, and Spike hung behind the horrified Princess Skystar. She looked so hurt and betrayed. Twilight felt awful for causing Skystar and the Seaponies distress, but she was still determined to get the one thing that would save the ponies of Equestria. Twilight reached out one last time....

FLASH! A blast of white light blinded her.

The next thing Twilight saw was the shore at the base of Mount Aris.

CHAPTER TWENTY

The bedraggled ponies rubbed the water out of their eyes as they peeled themselves from the ground. Once they were back on their hooves, they wasted no time. Applejack marched right up to Twilight and stomped her hoof in the sand. "What were you thinking?! I mean, stealing their pearl?"

"It was the only way to save Equestria!" Twilight explained.

"Except it *wasn't*!" Pinkie Pie added, her bottom lip jutting out in a pink pout. "The queen was going to say yes! We did what you told us, and that's what made her realize we were ponies worth saving." She began to pace around, thinking. She stopped dead in her tracks, coming to a realization. "Unless... you didn't really want us to show her the best time ever! You just wanted us to distract her!"

Everypony stared at Twilight in horror. Was it true?

Twilight let out a frustrated growl. "I never would have done it, but this isn't Equestria! We can't just dance around with con artists, make Rainbooms in the sky, and expect everything to work out! It's *not* enough; *we* are *not* enough!"

Pinkie Pie shook her sad pink mane. "No, Twilight. *We* stuck together. *We* were gonna get the help we needed. The only thing that stopped us was *you*."

This was ridiculous. Why couldn't Twilight's friends see that she was doing the best she could? The pressure of this entire situation was all on Twilight. She was the one Tempest Shadow was after, and she was the last princess of Equestria. "I'm the only one they want!"

"You're also the only one who doesn't trust her friends!" Pinkie Pie retorted. The other ponies nodded in agreement. Twilight wasn't being a team player.

That was enough. Twilight looked up to the spiky, desolate Mount Aris, and something snapped inside her. This was all too much, and her friends had been nothing but trouble for her. She spun around on her hooves and narrowed her eyes. "Well, maybe I would have been better off without *friends like you!*" Twilight yelled angrily. A spark of magical energy spit out of Twilight's horn, almost like Tempest's.

Twilight watched, but the sight of Pinkie Pie and the rest of her friends trotting away was blurry from the tears in her eyes. She had ruined everything by trying to steal the pearl. There was no way to save Equestria now. Twilight fell into a sad, crying heap of a pony. She didn't even notice the ominous dark clouds gathering above her.

At least Spike had hung back to make sure Twilight was okay. Or no one might have ever seen the princess get carted away in a cage by Tempest and her guards.

"Twilight!" Spike cried as his friend disappeared

into the hull of the skiff. He shot a sad blast of fire at the ship in a feeble attempt to do something to help. But it made no difference. Without her good friends, Princess Twilight Sparkle hadn't stood a chance. The ponies had been officially divided and conquered.

CHAPTER TWENTY-ONE

Tempest Shadow paced around Twilight's cage with pep in her step. It was the first time Twilight had seen her look anything resembling happy, which was very sad. "Aw, the Princess of Friendship..." Tempest chuckled. Her hooves clanked noisily on the floor. "With no friends! And no way out."

"Why are you doing this?" Twilight slumped down. "You're a pony! Just like me."

Tempest spun around. She cantered over to Twilight's cage and leaned in close enough for Twilight to see her broken horn. It was jagged and scarred. It looked so painful. "I'm nothing like you," Tempest growled with disdain. "I'm more than you'll ever be."

"Why are you so hateful?" Twilight's eyes searched Tempest's. "I don't understand...."

Maybe it was time Twilight Sparkle learned a little lesson and got some perspective on what it was like for somepony who hadn't had a perfect life like hers. She was just a little, pretty princess with every chance handed to her on a silver platter with cupcakes next to it.

"I once hoped for friendship, like you." Tempest took a deep breath. "But that was stupid and childish. Because, when things got difficult for me, my so-called pony 'friends' abandoned me."

Twilight's eyes grew large. "You had pony friends?"

"Of course I did," Tempest replied. "Fillies don't start out this way." She motioned to her broken horn and sneered. "But they certainly don't want to be around a Unicorn with a deformed horn. Even if they were playing in the forest with you when the ursa minor attacked, too." A tiny spark emitted from Tempest's horn. She hung her head low. "My friends didn't care about me after that. I was too revolting, and I couldn't play their little Unicorn games."

"I'm sorry you felt so alone," said Twilight tenderly. She put her hoof up to the bars of her cage to reach out for Tempest, who shrank away.

"I saw the truth. My 'friends' abandoned me when times got tough. Looks like I'm not the only one." Tempest smiled and began to trot to the door. She turned around and added one last sting before exiting. "Face it, Princess. Friendship has failed you, too."

Alone in her cage, Twilight realized the actual truth. Friendship hadn't failed her. Twilight had failed friendship. She'd grown selfish and put her friends in danger instead of working together to solve the problem, as she'd vowed she'd always do. And there was nothing Twilight could do about it now. The fate of Equestria was in somepony else's hooves now.

Hours later, Twilight was wheeled into the familiar castle throne room by fellow ponies with chains around their hooves. It was an awful feeling to enter her old home as a prisoner. But it was worse to see the other princesses frozen in stone and the Storm King sitting on the throne.

"Wow, it's a good thing they're stone, right? So you don't have to see their disappointment in your complete, utter failure." Tempest laughed.

Twilight whimpered at the nightmare. "Tempest, don't do this! Give the Storm King—"

"Your magic?" Tempest's horn crackled. "Did you think you'd keep it all to yourself? Time to share." The evil Unicorn smiled and looked out the window dreamily. "I'd love for everypony out there to know what I can *really* do!"

"*Oooh*, fascinating!" the Storm King bellowed. "Tell me, sparky, what *can* you do?! Light a little candle with that sparkler of yours?" He cackled at his nasty comment as if it were the funniest thing ever uttered. Tempest shrank back in embarrassment. Twilight again felt a tiny bit bad for her. The Storm King gestured his staff at Twilight. "Why is this one still moving?!"

Tempest gathered herself and remained professional. "She and her friends put up a bit of a fight, but she's alone now. She won't be a problem."

The Storm King lumbered across the room, looking around at the beautiful stained-glass windows and tapestries. "Yeah, so *speaking* of problems. This place. It seems...a little too—oh, I don't know—cute! I don't like cute; I never did like cute—doesn't really go with my whole big, bad, powerful-magic-guy thing, does it?! Deliver the punchline, Tempest, because this has gotta be a joke!"

The beast slammed his staff to the floor. Instantly, it began to rattle and shake with power as streams of magical energy started to sap from each princess statue. Twilight gritted her teeth, trying to resist the magical pull of the object, but it was so strong. Her horn sputtered and glowed as the magic swirled around the floor and rose to dance around the Storm King.

The staff glowed brightly. It was fully charged.

"Wow! Let's get this storm started!" he yelled with glee. "*Ooh*, hey, that's good—I should trademark that." He shot a jolt of energy at the wall, and it came crashing down. Debris flew across the room and into Twilight's cage. She ducked and squinted, feeling pain from the destruction of her beloved castle.

"Not bad. Actually, kind of first-rate! What else does it do?" he asked Tempest, admiring his new toy.

Tempest followed him and approached him meekly. "Your Excellency, you promised to restore my horn and give it even greater power—"

"You gotta be kidding me!" he interrupted, waving the staff around with reckless abandon. "I can move the *sun*?! *AH HAH HAH! Whoa*, and the moon!" The Storm King moved both heavenly bodies around in the sky, creating a continual, hyperfast dance of day and night.

"Day night, night day, night day night day night sunrise sunset…de de bup bup bup bah bah bah bah…"

the beast sang. Tempest looked annoyed and impatient. But Twilight realized all this dawdling could be useful. Maybe she still had time to come up with a plan.

If only her friends were with her.

CHAPTER TWENTY-TWO

Applejack, Rainbow Dash, Pinkie Pie, Fluttershy, and Rarity had been shocked when Spike came running breathlessly up to them to deliver the horrible news of Twilight's foalnapping. But it had been even more of a shock when Capper, Captain Celaeno, and Princess Skystar, transformed back into a Hippogriff, had appeared at Mount Aris shortly after, hoping to help the ponies. Once everycreature had been brought up to speed, they all seemed even more fired up and ready to take back Canterlot. The Storm King just couldn't go on terrorizing them—not without a fight! Plus, there was no chance they weren't going to save Twilight.

Between the cunning skills of Capper, the swash-buckling abilities of the pirates, and Princess Skystar's unwavering positivity and Hippogriff agility, the rag-tag team had been able to put together a solid plan for infiltrating the enemy headquarters.

And it was time.

When they arrived at Canterlot, two Storm Creature guards stood in front of Canterlot's main gates. They appeared to be of the standard oaf variety—fond of holding spears and grunting a lot, but that was about it. Capper adjusted his baker disguise, pushed his gigantic "cake" along, and smirked at his own genius. If this little plan didn't work, then he wasn't a cat named Capper. The ponies, who were bound in "shackles," with him really sold the whole story.

As soon as they got close, the guards blocked them with their spears. But Capper was unfazed. He pretended to consult his delivery clipboard.

"All right, then. Can one of y'all go and tell your boss he's not getting his 'Congratulations on subduing defenseless pastel ponies' cake?" Capper tapped his toe impatiently. "'Cause I don't want to be the one responsible for the big guy missing his special dessert, you know what I'm saying?"

The two guards looked at each other for an answer, shrugged, and stepped aside. It was working! Pinkie Pie couldn't help but smile as they trotted into Canterlot. It was easy as pie!

"Pinkie, quit lookin' so happy! Y'ain't foolin' nopony!" Applejack barked under her breath.

Pinkie nodded and put on a dramatic sad face for the rest of the trip to the center of Canterlot. The plan was to go straight to the castle and attack from the inside, but once they'd arrived at the main plaza, Grubber happened to see the giant cake. The treat-loving creature ambled over greedily.

"Hello, cake!" he said, climbing onto the cart to snag a taste of the confection. "Don't mind if I do." His little paw grabbed a fistful of icing and cake, revealing a set of eyes behind it! "Who puts eyeballs in filling?" he wondered aloud.

Before he could call for the guards, a gaggle of

giant birds sprang from the cake! They burst forth and lunged for the Storm Creatures, entangling themselves in a full-on battle! Skystar, in Hippogriff form, accompanied Pinkie Pie and the other ponies, flinging cupcake ammo and taking out several Storm Creatures on their own. The entire kingdom looked like a big mess of hooves, fur, and feathers, and soon the Storm Creatures were retreating in fear from the ferocious band of ragtag scalawags!

Capper had done it. They had begun to take back Canterlot.

CHAPTER TWENTY-THREE

The commotion down below reached up to the tallest towers of the castle. When they heard the sounds of the Storm Creatures surrendering, Tempest Shadow darted from the throne room to the balcony in disbelief. "What?!" she cried, watching the destruction. "How?!"

Twilight gasped. "It's...it's the Magic of—"

"Yeah, yeah!" the Storm King mocked, making his voice high-pitched and silly. He leaned down and pulled Tempest and a freshly uncaged, but magic-less Twilight into an insincere embrace. "Friendship and flowers and ponies and...*bleeeehhhhh!*" He straightened up, a menacing look in his eyes. "I'm so totally over the cute-pony thing!" The Storm King raised his staff to the darkening sky. *"THIS ENDS NOW!"*

A zap of lightning shot straight up from the end of the staff to the heavens. The black clouds moved in, covering the entire sky above Canterlot. A whoosh of wind barreled through, kicking up dust and twisting it into a gigantic tornado. "Yeah!" The Storm King cackled. He was a maniac! And he had nothing in the world to lose.

Twilight wanted to do something, but it was as if her hooves were frozen in place. With the Staff of Sacanas under his control, the Storm King was so powerful. All Twilight was managing to do was look on in horror as her home was about to be destroyed.

On the ground below, Capper and the crew ran for cover. "Move your hooves, ponies!" he shouted as the tornado began to pick up Storm Creatures and all kinds of other debris.

Rainbow Dash couldn't tear her eyes away from

the twister. "You'd have to be faster than a speeding Pegasus to break through *that* wind!"

Pinkie's eyes widened with intrigue. "Excellent idea, Rainbow Dash!" She whipped out a helmet and secured it over her curly fuchsia mane. If there was ever a time to attempt something like this, it was now. All Pinkie had to do was find some helpers first....

The sound of the Storm King's booming voice echoed right through the chaos. "Now I truly am the Storm King!" He threw his hairy white arms out in triumph. "And the entire world will bow to my va va va *VOOM, BABY*!" His laughter pierced Tempest's ears, and she shuddered. She had endured his behavior with no compensation long enough. It was her time now.

The plum pony stepped forward to make her case. "Yes, yes, you are every bit as powerful as I promised, sire. Now, restore my horn and I swear to use my magic to serve you!" She bent her foreleg and bowed down to the beast. But her request was met with maniacal cackles.

"Who cares about your dinky little Unicorn horn?!" the Storm King bellowed. He pushed Tempest aside as if she were yesterday's trash.

Tempest shook her head in disbelief. Tears began to well up in her eyes. "But we had an agreement...."

"Get with the program." His broad chest bounced up and down as he laughed. "I *used* you. It's kinda what I do!" The Storm King raised his staff and pointed it at Tempest. Blasts of magical energy shot toward her, and the pony stumbled back, straight into the tornado! Tempest grabbed on to the balcony railing and gripped it for dear life, but it was no use. It was a fitting end for a pathetic, useless Unicorn without a horn or a single friend in the world.

This would be the last of Tempest Shadow.

CHAPTER TWENTY-FOUR

Hold on!" Twilight Sparkle shouted over the roar of the worsening storm. Tempest may have been working against her and all Equestria this entire time, but there was no way Twilight could stand by and watch this happen to the other Unicorn. The princess galloped over and reached her hoof out to her captor.

Tempest's big aqua eyes searched Twilight's. "Why are you saving me?"

"Because this...is what friends do!" Twilight reached both hooves out to Tempest and yanked her back onto the balcony. The ponies tumbled to the surface with an unceremonious crash.

By the time the two ponies picked themselves off the floor, the Storm King was back. He towered over them, pointing the staff directly at their terrified faces. But he was interrupted by a strange sound.

"Wheeeeeeeeeeee!" A shrill shriek of excitement rang out. Pinkie Pie, Applejack, Fluttershy, Rainbow Dash, Rarity, and Spike came barreling through the air right toward the balcony! They knocked the staff out of the Storm King's claw, sending it clattering into the other room as they landed in an ungraceful heap. Everypony groaned in pain except Pinkie. She immediately sprang to her hooves and shouted triumphantly. "Bull's-eye!"

"You all came back!" Twilight rushed over. She had never been so glad to see her friends. She began to replay in her mind the events that had led them here. "I'm *so* sorry! I was wrong to—"

Pinkie gave her a sad smile. "I'm sorry, too. Friends mess up sometimes, but we never should—"

"Uh, make up later?!" Rainbow Dash flew over them in a panic. "This isn't over!" She gestured to the Storm King, who had scrambled inside the throne room. The staff was now lodged in the stained-glass window. It was wildly out of control, sending even stronger zaps of lightning magic across the space. It shot a blast at the ceiling, and chunks of marble and stone began to shatter and fall around them. The ponies darted out of the way of the falling debris, permanent looks of horror and panic on their faces.

"I've got to get control of it!" Twilight shouted, moving in closer. The strong winds whipped her mane around. Time was running out before her beloved Canterlot would crumble to dust.

"You've got this, Twilight," Pinkie shouted over the strengthening storm. Applejack nodded in support.

"No!" Twilight puffed out her chest. "*We've* got this. Together." Of course—the friends had always been stronger as a unit than individually. Now was no different. Twilight reached for Pinkie's hoof, and instantly the ponies were transformed into a powerful chain, swaying in the strong winds. The strength of Applejack's lasso tethered them to the ground.

It was working!

Now when she reached out her hoof, Twilight could almost reach the staff!

"The staff belongs to *me!*" the hairy beast bellowed as he scrambled over the stones. The window began to crack from the magical pressure, due to shatter at any second. "The power is mine!" The Storm King made one last sad attempt to seize the staff by hurling himself at the weakening glass.

But the storm was way too strong. The glass shattered and sucked Twilight and the Storm King into the vortex of scary, violent winds. *"Noooo!"* Pinkie Pie cried out in anguish for her friend.

Twilight was gone! This couldn't be happening.

✦✦ CHAPTER TWENTY-FIVE ✦✦

A blinding flash of light pierced through the clouds, and with it, a calm washed over Canterlot. The storm was over. Everything was still, but the ponies couldn't tear their eyes away from the spot where Twilight had disappeared. Fluttershy's eyes were wet with tears as she exchanged a look with a distraught Rarity. Their best friend couldn't be gone forever... could she? The idea was almost too much to bear.

Then, from high above, Twilight appeared with the staff! She was the picture of a princess—regal and serene. Everypony cheered as Twilight descended and was immediately enveloped in a group hug. Tempest hung back nearby, watching their friendship with wonder. Before Twilight had saved her, Tempest couldn't imagine feeling the way they all did about one another. Now she understood.

Tempest was the first to see the Storm King pulling himself up onto the balcony. "I'm not done yet!" he mumbled under his breath. The ponies were so distracted that they didn't notice him pulling out a spare Obsidian Orb and gearing up to throw it at Twilight.

"Nooooo!" Tempest shouted as she leaped over the ponies and straight into the line of fire. Once the orb made contact, it exploded in a dramatic cloud of magical smoke. Tempest and the Storm King both froze in midair as their bodies turned completely into stone.

Unable to move, the Storm King fell back over the edge of the balcony and crashed to the ground below. The stone broke apart into a thousand tiny pieces. But Tempest was frozen and caught in a magic bubble, surrounded by the glittering purple magic of Twilight's horn. The princess lowered her gently onto the balcony.

Rainbow Dash shook her head in sheer amazement. "Whoa, I can't believe she did that!"

"I can," Twilight said, unable to hide her proud smile. The princess grabbed on to the staff and encouraged her friends to do the same. All six ponies and Spike shared the weight of it, pointing the powerful beam directly at Tempest.

Slowly, the Unicorn's body returned to its normal color. Tempest was able to move once more. The look of surprise on her face said everything. Tempest was new to this whole friendship thing, but Princess Twilight Sparkle had a feeling she was going to like it.

"Now what?" Fluttershy wondered aloud.

"Now we fix everything," Twilight said, feeling hopeful. Her home was not ruined. The magic from the staff was powerful enough to undo all the destruction the Storm King had caused. And that's exactly what Twilight did.

CHAPTER TWENTY-SIX

Canterlot was looking gorgeous, thanks to the helping hooves of everypony in the kingdom. There wasn't a single cloud in the sky, and the sun shone down on the Friendship Festival stage, lighting it with a golden glow that even magic couldn't create. The throngs of ponies stomped their hooves in excitement as the small Dragon took to the stage.

"Fillies and gentlecolts!" Spike shouted to the huge crowd. "Get ready for a little...Songbird Serenade!"

The pop star gave a big smile and waved. "And now to celebrate that we're all still here in one piece—give it up for Princess Twilight and her friends!" She motioned over to where Twilight, Rarity, Applejack, Fluttershy,

Rainbow Dash, Pinkie Pie, and Spike stood together off to the side of the stage. The ponies blushed at the sound of deafening applause and cheering.

As the party raged on throughout the afternoon and well into the evening, the spirit of the festival could be seen everywhere. Friends new and old were busy having fun together. Capper and Rarity chatted about her surprise gift to him (a new coat); Pinkie Pie and Princess Skystar shared cupcakes and giggles; and Rainbow Dash and her new pal, Captain Celaeno, exchanged stories of awesomeness and adventures. Spike was getting along surprisingly well with Grubber, and Queen Novo even joined the celebration with some of her Hippogriff friends!

There was only one little pony who didn't seem to be enjoying herself. Twilight trotted over to Tempest and gave her a smile.

"That's one thing that never changes around here: a party."

"Well, I hope you'll stay," Twilight said warmly. "More friends are definitely merrier!"

Tempest slumped down with a heavy sigh. "But what about my broken horn?" Her voice wilted the tiniest bit when she said it. Even with all the merriment around her, Tempest was still hung up on something that made her special.

"You know," Twilight said, "your horn is pretty powerful, just like the pony it belongs to."

At this, a hint of a genuine smile began to form on Tempest's face. Nopony had ever complimented her broken horn before. It could do some unique things. Maybe it was time to share them.

"I've been wanting to show everypony in Equestria what I can do," Tempest conceded. She summoned her magical strength and shot off some crackling sparks from her horn. They zoomed up high into the sky and exploded into the most brilliant, fizzling fireworks!

"Nice touch, Tempest!" Pinkie Pie called out as she bounced over. Fluttershy trotted behind her.

"Actually, that's not my real name," Tempest said with a sheepish shrug.

"Ooooh!" Pinkie Pie squealed. "What is it?"

Applejack, Rarity, and Rainbow Dash trotted over and crowded in, hoping to hear as well. Tempest really was a pony of mystery! She motioned for them all to get closer before whispering, "Uh, my real name is... Fizzlepop Berrytwist." Tempest's eyes were wide with embarrassment.

"*Okay!*" Pinkie Pie gasped. "That is the most awesome name *ever*!"

Everypony erupted into giggles and nodded in agreement. For the first time in forever, Tempest Shadow joined in, too. She may have forgotten what the Magic of Friendship felt like, but she never would again.

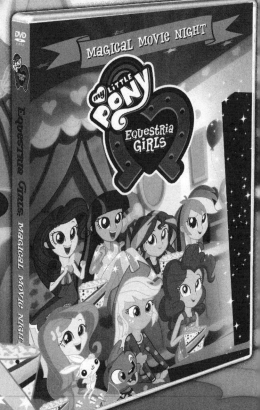